MY FIRST
I Can Read Book®

Biscuit

story by Alyssa Satin Capucilli
pictures by Pat Schories

HarperCollins*Publishers*

HarperCollins®, ♛®, and I Can Read Book®
are trademarks of HarperCollins Publishers Inc.

Biscuit
Text copyright © 1996 by Alyssa Satin Capucilli
Illustrations copyright © 1996 by Pat Schories
Printed in the U.S.A. All rights reserved.

Library of Congress Cataloging-in-Publication Data
Capucilli, Alyssa Satin
   Biscuit/ story by Alyssa Satin Capucilli ; pictures by Pat Schories.
      p.   cm. — (My first I can read book)
   Summary: A little yellow dog wants ever one more thing before he'll go to sleep.
   ISBN 0-06-026197-8. — ISBN 0-06-026198-6 (lib. bdg.)
   [1. Dogs—Fiction.   2. Bedtime—Fiction.]   I. Schories, Pat, ill.
II. Title.   III. Series.
PZ7.C179Bi   1996   95-9716
[E]—dc20   CIP
                                                                              AC

❖
Reprinted by arrangement with HarperCollins Publishers.
10 9 8 7

For Laura and Peter who wait patiently
for a Biscuit of their very own
—A. S. C.

For Tess
—P. S.

This is Biscuit.

Biscuit is small.

Biscuit is yellow.

Time for bed, Biscuit!

Woof, woof!

Biscuit wants to play.

Time for bed, Biscuit!

Woof, woof!

Biscuit wants a snack.

Time for bed, Biscuit!

Woof, woof!

Biscuit wants a drink.

Time for bed, Biscuit!

Woof, woof!

Biscuit wants to hear a story.

Time for bed, Biscuit!

Woof, woof!

Biscuit wants his blanket.

Time for bed, Biscuit!

Woof, woof!

Biscuit wants his doll.

Time for bed, Biscuit!

Woof, woof!

Biscuit wants a hug.

Time for bed, Biscuit!

Woof, woof!

Biscuit wants a kiss.

Time for bed, Biscuit!

Woof, woof!

Biscuit wants a light on.

Woof!

Biscuit wants to be tucked in.

Woof!

Biscuit wants one more kiss.

Woof!

Biscuit wants one more hug.

Woof!

Biscuit wants to curl up.

Sleepy puppy.

Good night, Biscuit.